KT-386-205

©1990 Grandreams Limited
This edition published in 1997

The Little Toy Theatre, Sam's Special Sandwiches, The Dog Who Fetched Father Christmas, The No-Snowman, The Little Rabbit And The Forgetful Elf written by Valerie Hall. Santa's Ride, Santa's Best Coat, Wildlife In Winter, Colin And The Gnomes' Circus, Gina The Giddy Giraffe, Olly Octopus And The Sea King's Treasure, Selena And The Dream Weaver's Thread written by Beryl Johnston.

Illustrations by Linden Artists: Cover, The Little Toy Theatre, Santa's Ride, Wildlife In Winter, Gina The Giddy Giraffe, The Little Rabbit And The Forgetful Elf, Olly Octopus And The Sea King's Treasure, The Night Before Christmas, Russell and Russell: The Dog Who Fetched Father Christmas, The No-Snowman, Santa's Best Coat. Temple Rogers: Colin And The Gnomes' Circus, Selena And The Dream Weaver's Thread. Associated Freelance Artists: Sam's Special Sandwiches.

Published by
Grandreams Limited
435-437 Edgware Road, Little Venice, London, W2 ITH

Printed in Hong Kong

XM5

CONTENTS

The Little Toy Theatre

"That!" exclaimed Mr. Penrose, pushing his chair away from the table and pulling out his napkin from under his chin, "was a perfectly splendid Christmas dinner."

His wife smiled. "Thank you, dear, but it's not over yet. There are tangerines and nuts to follow."

Mr. Penrose groaned. "If so much as a segment of orange or a tiny walnut passed my lips I'd burst all my buttons on my new waistcoat." And he puffed himself to show everyone what might happen, which the children, George, Elizabeth and Anne, found most amusing.

Mrs Penrose rang for the maid to come and clear away, then the family made its way into the parlour. Mr. Penrose promptly collapsed into his favourite armchair and the children set about playing with the presents they had opened that morning.

George emptied a box of shiny, red-uniformed, metal soldiers onto the floor and began setting them out. "Will you be the blue army, Father, so that I can have a battle?"

Mr. Penrose had been planning to have a quiet snooze, but he cheerfully lowered himself onto his knees and lined up the blue-coated opposition.

Elizabeth had been given a toy sewing machine for Christmas and was planning to make her dolls a new wardrobe of clothes.

"You will help me, won't you?" she begged her mother.

On hearing this, little Anne quickly looked up. "But you promised you'd help me," she whined. "You know I can't do it on my own, it's much too hard." Her present was a toy theatre made of card, complete with scenery, actors and a play to perform. Unfortunately for Anne, it all had to be cut out and stuck together before she could play with it.

"I know I said I'd help you," said her mother, "and so I shall, as soon as I've cut out something for Elizabeth to sew. Now be a good girl and bring me my workbox."

Slowly the little theatre began to take shape. George left the battle he was fighting to fix the stage together. Elizabeth put aside the party frock she was making for her best doll to help her sister cut out the characters and stick them to long strips of card with which they could be moved about. When it was finished, Anne was eager to put on a show.

"I think you ought to practise first," suggested her mother.

"Of course," said Anne. "But you don't practise - you rehearse."

George and Elizabeth wanted to join in. "Which play shall we do?" they asked.

"'Sleeping Beauty'," said Anne.

George groaned. "Why, there are hardly any fights or battles in 'Sleeping Beauty'."

"Good!" chorused the sisters. Then the threesome huddled together behind the sofa to rehearse.

After tea, Mr. and Mrs Penrose, Cook and Sarah, the maid, were called into the parlour and shown where to sit. Elizabeth played a little tune on the piano then joined her brother and sister behind a table on which was set a toy theatre. The curtain was about to go up.

Apart from some scenery getting stuck and one or two of the actors falling over, the first part of the play went well. First there was the christening, where the wicked fairy puts a curse on the baby Princess, followed by the sixteenth birthday party, where the Princess pricks her finger and falls asleep for a hundred years.

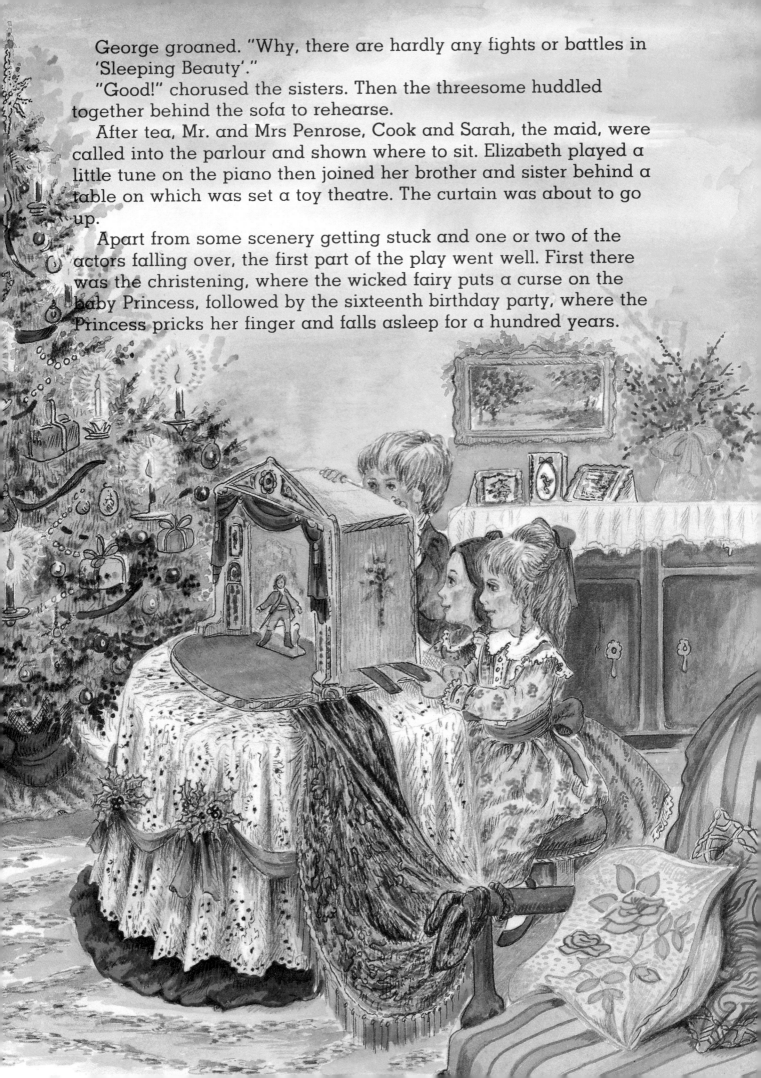

It was where the Prince meets a character called Ogre
Frostytoes that things started to go wrong. George, who was doing
their voices and moving them, thought that things needed livening
up.

"Take that, you ugly ogre," said the Prince, jabbing the ogre
with his sword.

"I'm not ugly," growled Ogre Frostytoes, jumping up and down
on the Prince. None of it was in the script.

Anne was horrified. "Stop it," she cried. "Stop it at once. You're
messing everything up. Oh, please tell him to stop, Father."

Mr. Penrose was trying not to laugh. "Now that's enough,
George. If you're not careful you'll do some damage."

But it was too late. The little toy theatre had already begun to
come apart. George saw what was happening and stopped.

"I am sorry, Anne," he said. "I didn't mean to do that. I can stick it together again. You'll see."

Anne wasn't listening. She had fled to the nursery in tears and, even though it was Christmas, that was where she stayed for the rest of the day.

When Anne opened her eyes the next morning the first thing she saw was the toy theatre sitting on the table at the end of her bed. George, who'd been waiting for her to wake up, popped his head round the door. "It's as good as new, Anne, I promise you. Er, you're not still cross with me, are you?" he asked, anxiously.

Anne gave a weak smile and tried to shake her head, but it hurt. Her throat hurt too and her eyes felt hot. George called his parents who hurried to the nursery.

"She has a slight temperature," said Mrs Penrose, "but I don't

think we need call for the doctor. We'll keep her in bed today and see how she is tomorrow."

"What about tonight?" whispered Mr. Penrose. "What about the pantomime?" His wife shook her head and he gave a sigh. He had planned a surprise trip to see a real production of 'Sleeping Beauty' and he knew how disappointed Anne would be.

Anne was disappointed, but she tried not to show it when her brother and sister popped in to say goodnight before they left for the theatre. "It probably won't be half as good as my toy theatre," she joked. But when they had gone, she thought about them, dressed in their best clothes waiting for the thrilling moment when the curtain would rise and the play begin, and two tears trickled down her cheeks and plopped onto the eiderdown.

She dozed for a while and then something made her open her eyes and look at the little theatre. It seemed different, as though it was lit up and the Fairy Queen, who was standing in the centre of the stage, didn't look like a paper cut-out at all, she looked real. When she started to speak, Anne knew that she was.

"Quiet and still! Do not make a sound!
Wherever I am there is magic around.
A tale I will conjure of a King and a Queen,
Their daughter; a Princess, the loveliest ever seen.
Of good and of evil and a Prince, oh so bold!
So with no more ado, let our story unfold!"

And unfold it did. Anne watched her little cut-out players
perform 'Sleeping Beauty' for her eyes alone. And finally, when the
Prince woke the Princess with a kiss, Anne drifted off into a deep,
peaceful sleep.

The next day Anne was feeling much better.

"I didn't miss the pantomime after all," she told her family. "The little people in my toy theatre came alive and did 'Sleeping Beauty' just for me."

"That's funny," said Mr. Penrose, "the people we saw in 'Sleeping Beauty' were just like the cardboard cut-outs."

George sniggered at his father's joke. "But it's true, Anne insisted. "When George put my theatre there yesterday, the Fairy Queen was alone on the stage, now there's the King and Queen and Sleeping Beauty and the Prince too."

"Perhaps you put them there and then forgot," suggested Elizabeth.

"No, I didn't," said Anne, starting to get tearful.

Mrs Penrose intervened. "If Anne said it happened, then it happened. We'll let her get some rest and perhaps she'll be well enough to come downstairs for lunch. There's cold turkey, Christmas pudding and trifle - your favourite."

When everyone had gone, Anne clambered to the bottom of her bed and picked up some of her cut-out characters. They seemed so lifeless in her hand that she was beginning to think she had dreamt it all. Then she noticed something glinting in a corner of the stage. She picked it up and a shiver of excitement ran through her whole body for she held between her fingers the tiniest of silver needles. It was much smaller than any in her mother's workbox and just like the one on which Sleeping Beauty pricked her finger in the play!

Wildlife In Winter

It's funny, when you walk around
And think of creatures underground,
So many sleeping safe and sound
In burrow deep or earthy mound.

The badger in his set will sleep
And only out with dusk he'll creep,
The fox into his lair can leap
While hedgehogs tight till Spring will keep;

And stranger when you think, instead,
Of creatures living overhead,
How cosily they lie abed
When trees and bushes look so dead.

The squirrel nestles in his drey.
The owl will slumber through the day
While rooks on higher branches sway
And finches in the thornbush play.

They do not have the kind of heat
We need to warm our hands and feet,
For cosy fur is hard to beat
And feathers are both warm and neat.

They gather leaves with beak and claw
Or bracken dry, with mouth and paw,
To line their dwelling, roof to floor
And keep them safe through Winter raw.

Sam's Special Sandwiches

When Sam Stevens got home from school he knew right away that something was wrong; his dad's car was in the drive and Dad was never home that early. He threw a breathless "thank you" to the lady who had driven him home and dashed up to the front door. It opened before Sam could ring the bell and Mr. Stevens was standing there, smiling. "Bet you're surprised to see me," he said.

Sam went in, hung up his coat and satchel, and looked round for his mother; she wasn't there. A horrid tingly feeling came into his stomach.

Mr. Stevens crouched down and put his hands on Sam's shoulders.

"Granny's hurt her foot and can't walk very well so Mummy's staying with her for a few days to help out."

"Whew!" sighed Sam, relieved that things weren't as bad as he'd imagined. The tingly feeling in his tummy went away.

"Why don't you go upstairs and wash your hands while I make your tea?" suggested Sam's dad. "And what will M'sewer 'ave?" he asked in a funny accent. "Lobstaire Sooflay? Duck with a beeootiful orange soos? Or plain old Caviar and cheeps?"

Sam laughed and settled for fish fingers and tinned spaghetti. He was well aware that his dad could barely boil an egg.

After tea Sam made his Granny a 'get well' card and then watched TV.

"Bath time, Sam," came a voice from the kitchen. His dad was still trying to clean spaghetti off the bottom of the pan.

Sam was on his way upstairs when he remembered something that brought a funny feeling back into his tummy and sent him hurrying down again.

"What's the matter?" said his dad, as Sam burst into the kitchen.

"Tomorrow. It's the school Christmas party."

His dad frowned. "So?"

"We're all supposed to take something to eat. Mum said she'd make me some sandwiches and a cake."

"I see," said Mr. Stevens, and thought for a minute. "Well I don't know about the cake, but I'm sure I could manage the sandwiches."

"Perhaps I'd better help," said Sam, doubtfully.

"All right then. I'll butter, you spread."

While his dad buttered slices of bread, Sam got out all his favourite fillings; peanut butter, cheese spread, honey, jam and chicken paste. To these he added a jar of gherkins and a jar of little white onions.

With all the buttered bread spread out on the table, Sam went round putting on a bit of this, a bit of that, a gherkin here, an onion there until half the slices were covered. Then he put on the tops.

Mr. Stevens eyed them curiously. "What's in that one?" he asked.

Sam lifted its lid. "Cheese spread, honey and gherkin," he said, proudly.

His dad grinned. "Seeing that they're such *unusual* sandwiches, why don't we cut them into unusual shapes instead of boring old squares and triangles? We could use Mummy's pastry cutters."

Sam thought this was a great idea and when they finished there were hearts, rounds, diamonds and curly shaped sandwiches all over the place.

Inglenook Infants was in a state of high excitement for not only was it the day of the Christmas party, but a very special visitor was coming as well.

Sam carefully carried his tray of sandwiches to his classroom and put them on a table with all the other food. The room looked jolly with paper chains hanging from the ceiling, cut out stars stuck to the windows and a crib in the corner with Jesus, Mary and Joseph made out of Plasticene; the children had done it all themselves.

Most of the day was spent playing games in the big hall while the teachers laid out the food ready for the party. At two-thirty it was to begin.

When Sam and his classmates got back they all gasped. It didn't look like their classroom anymore. Their little tables were covered with bright red paper and there were hats and streamers tucked in between the plates of food. And what food! Sandwiches, sausage rolls, crisps, cakes, jellies, biscuits and orange squash to drink.

"All right, children, dig in," yelled Mrs Peel, their teacher.

A big cheer went up and twenty or so little boys and girls 'dug in' to the feast.

Sam was pleased to see that everyone went for the sandwiches first. They liked the funny shapes. But then one little girl, who'd taken a bite from a heart shaped one, started coughing.

"Ugh! These are terrible. They've got bits in."

"Yuk! So has mine," said another.

Three or four more started to cough and splutter and Mrs Peel had to run round with the waste paper bin for them to spit out in. Sam felt that nasty tingle again.

Mrs Peel caught sight of his face. "Don't cry, dear," she begged. "Not now. We don't want to spoil the party."

Sam didn't cry. He was about to when the door was thrown open by the headmistress and in walked a very special visitor.

Mrs Peel curtsied. The visitor smiled and strolled around looking at the paintings and models and talking to some of the children as she went.

Stopping by Sam's table she pointed to his sandwiches.

"Those look nice. May I have one?" she asked.

Mrs Peel made a move to stop her but the visitor had already taken a bite. Everyone watched as she chewed, swallowed, frowned and then looked surprised. Mrs Peel picked up the waste paper bin, just in case.

The visitor opened her mouth . . . and spoke.

"Peanut butter?"

Sam nodded.

"Little white onions? Jam?"

Sam nodded again.

The very important visitor beamed. "My favourite sandwich filling. How did you know?"

The tingly feeling left Sam's tummy for once and for all. And after the visitor had gone, everyone wanted one of Sam's special sandwiches. But Sam politely said "no" and took them home to share with his dad for tea.

Colin and The Gnomes' Circus

Colin was riding down the lane on his bike when a rabbit came running out of the hedge and along the road in front of him. Colin stopped and blinked, because on the rabbit's back was a small saddle, and on his head was a bridle with bells that jingled as he bobbed along.

Then through the hedge scrambled a small gnome, dressed in a red coat with shiny buttons and a small top hat. "Did you see a circus rabbit come past?" he gasped.

"Yes, he went that way," pointed Colin. "Get on my bike and I'll try to catch up with him."

The gnome ringmaster hopped on the back of Colin's bike and they sped down the lane. "There he is," whispered Colin, spotting the rabbit which had stopped to nibble some grass.

The gnome crept towards the rabbit and grabbed his bridle. "Thanks for your help," he said to Colin. "Everything is going wrong today. The performing hedgehogs have gone all sulky and rolled up in prickly balls, and we have to give a special show this afternoon.

"I didn't know hedgehogs could do tricks," said Colin.

"Oh yes, they are very clever at juggling. They can throw apples into the air and catch them on their spines. But they won't perform today and I don't know what act I can put on in their place."

The ringmaster led Colin through the hedge and in a large field on the other side was the gnomes' circus. There were brightly painted caravans round a big tent. Flags were flying from the top and over the entrance, on a big board with light bulbs all round it, was written: GNOMES CIRCUS. A small pixie girl rushed up to the rabbit and stroked his nose, before leading him towards the tent.

Inside the tent the circus performers were rehearsing. There were gnomes on the tightrope, gnome acrobats, badgers who did a balancing act and some clever squirrel trapeze artists.

"Where are the clowns?" asked Colin.

"Clowns?" said the ringmaster. "We haven't any of those. What are they like?"

"You can't have a proper circus without a clown," declared Colin. "Look, I'll show you."

He searched in his pockets for some pieces of coloured chalk. First he smothered his face with white chalk, then he drew some funny lines on his nose, eyes and cheeks with a red piece. Then he put on his coat and cap back-to-front. The gnome ringmaster laughed so much that all the other circus performers came crowding round. "You must take part in our special show," they told him.

Very soon the big tent began to fill with gnomes who had come to see the show.

When the band started playing, Colin jumped on his bike and rode into the circus ring. Then he jumped off and turned a somersault. After that he ran round the ring and pretended to trip, falling flat on his face. All the gnomes in the crowd laughed as he picked himself up.

Moving towards some buckets of water he'd told the ringmaster to place near the performers' entrance, Colin picked up one and ran into the ring again, tripping

and spilling the water. While the audience was roaring with laughter, he fetched another, and the same thing happened. The gnomes thought this was really funny.

Then he grabbed a third bucket and took it right across the ring to the gnomes sitting in the best seats. How they squealed as Colin swung back the bucket, expecting water was going to be thrown right over them. And how everybody laughed when they saw the bucket was empty.

Colin turned three somersaults and ran out of the ring. But he had to go back and take a special bow because the gnomes all clapped so much.

"The hedgehogs were watching you from their secret hiding place under the seats," the ringmaster told Colin, after the show. "You made them laugh so much, they've stopped sulking. Now they've agreed to do their act again, but I wish you could stay with our circus."

"So do I," replied Colin. "But perhaps I can be a real clown again, one day!"

The Night Before Christmas

'Twas the night before Christmas,
   when all through the house
Not a creature was stirring,
   not even a mouse;
The stockings were hung
   by the chimney with care,
In hopes that St. Nicholas
   soon would be there;
The children were nestled
   all snug in their beds,
While visions of sugar-plums
   danced in their heads;
And Mamma in her kerchief,
   and I in my cap,
Had just settled our brains
   For a long winter's nap;

When out on the lawn
   there arose such a clatter,
I sprang from the bed
   to see what was the matter.
Away to the window
   I flew like a flash,
Tore open the shutters,
   and threw up the sash.
The moon on the breast
   of the new-fallen snow,
Gave the lustre of midday
   to objects below;
When, what to my wondering
   eyes should appear,
But a miniature sleigh
   and eight tiny reindeer,
With a little old driver,
   so lively and quick,
I knew in a moment,
   it must be St. Nick.

More rapid than eagles
 his coursers they came,
And he whistled, and shouted,
 and called them by name:
"Now, Dasher! now, Dancer!
 now, Prancer and Vixen!
On, Comet! on, Cupid!
 on, Donner and Blitzen!
To the top of the porch!
 to the top of the wall!

Now dash away! dash away!
 dash away all!"
As dry leaves that before
 the wild hurricane fly,
When they meet with an obstacle,
 mount to the sky,
So up to the house-top
 the coursers they flew,
With the sleigh full of toys,
 and St. Nicholas too.
And then in a twinkle,
 I heard on the roof,
The prancing and pawing,
 of each little hoof.
As I drew in my head,
 and was turning around,

Down the chimney St. Nicholas
    came with a bound.
He was dressed all in fur,
    from his head to his foot,
And his clothes were all tarnished
    with ashes and soot;
A bundle of toys
    he flung on his back,
And he looked like a pedlar
    just opening his pack.
His eyes - how they twinkled!
    his dimples how merry!
His cheeks were like roses,
    his nose like a cherry!
His droll little mouth
    was drawn like a bow,
And the beard on his chin
    was as white as the snow;

The stump of a pipe
   he held tight in his teeth,
And the smoke it encircled
   his head like a wreath;
He had a broad face
   and a little round belly,
That shook when he laughed,
   like a bowful of jelly.
He was chubby and plump -
   a right jolly old elf -
And I laughed when I saw him,
   in spite of myself.
A wink in his eye
   and a twist of his head,
Soon gave me to know
   I had nothing to dread.
He spoke not a word,
   but went straight to his work,
And filled all the stockings;
   then turned with a jerk,
And laying his finger
   aside of his nose,
And giving a nod,
   up the chimney he rose;
He sprang to his sleigh,
   to his team gave a whistle,
And away they all flew
   like the down of a thistle.
But I heard him exclaim,
   ere he drove out of sight,
"Happy Christmas to all,
   and to all a good night!"

SELENA & THE DREAM WEAVER'S THREAD

Once, long ago, a weaver set up his loom in a market place. Fascinated, the people of the town came crowding round to watch him at work.

They gasped in wonder when they saw the beautiful cloth he was weaving, for it was full of lovely colours and shone like the sun. "Who are you, and what are you weaving?" they asked.

"I am a dream weaver," he told

them. "If you take a piece of this cloth and lay it on your pillow tonight, you will have the most wonderful dreams."

The news quickly spread around the town until it reached the King's palace. Soon a great, golden coach was seen coming into the square. "It's the King himself!" cried the townspeople and they made way for him as he walked towards the loom.

"What price is your cloth?" he asked.

"One piece of gold for every dream," said the weaver.

So the King's Chamberlain handed the weaver a piece of gold. Then he laid the cloth the weaver gave him on a special silk cushion. "Tonight I will place that cushion under my head," said the King, as he drove off in his gold coach.

Then all the townspeople began to buy the cloth as fast as the weaver could fill his loom. Everyone who had a piece of gold came running to buy.

Behind them all came a very poor girl whose name was Selena. She was a begger-maid and had no gold. She had only a penny with which she was going to buy a little bread for her supper.

"What price is your dream cloth?" she asked the weaver.

"One piece of gold," the weaver replied. "But you are too late. I don't have enough thread to weave another dream."

"And I have only one penny," said Selena, sadly.

"There is one tiny piece of thread left," the weaver showed her. "You may have that for a penny."

So Selena gave him her penny and took the small piece of glittering thread. "Perhaps I may have just one little raggedy dream with this," she said. So she ran through the town to her tumbledown house in a narrow street.

As she ran she tripped and fell, and tore the skirt of her thin dress. "Oh, dear," she shivered. "I must mend this." But the only thread she could find was the piece she had just bought from the dream weaver.

So she set to work and mended her dress. "I shall not have even a raggedy dream, after all," she sighed, as she laid her head on a bundle of straw and soon fell asleep.

High on the hill, in the royal palace, the King called for his silken pillow with the dream weaver's cloth laid on it. "If the weaver's words are true, tonight I will have a most wonderful dream,"

he delcared.

The King fell asleep and began to dream. It was a wonderful dream, but very strange. He dreamt he was riding in his golden coach through a part of town that he had never seen before. The streets were dark and narrow, and the houses small and tumbledown. As he passed one house a beautiful girl stepped from the door, dressed in a lovely gown.

Then the King woke up. It was already morning and the sun was just rising. "What a strange dream," he cried. "I wonder if it will come true? I must search the town and see if I can find a Princess living in such an unlikely place."

He called for his golden coach and began to search through all the streets in the town.

At that moment, Selena the begger-maid was waking too. She had not dreamed at all, but her dark little room seemed brighter than usual. She looked at her dress and rubbed her eyes in amazement. During the night the dream weaver's thread had changed it into a beautiful gown. It was full of lovely colours and shone like the sun and sparkled like the stars. It was the most beautiful dress she had ever seen.

Selena put it on and then she heard the sound of horses and people shouting in the street outside. Quickly, she ran to the door to see what was happening.

The King was just passing in his coach. "Stop!" he cried, as Selena appeared. "Here is my Princess, just as I saw her in my dream."

He jumped from his coach and knelt at her feet, and asked her to be his Queen. And because she knew it must be part of the dream magic, Selena said: "Yes!"

So the King took Selena in the golden coach, back to the palace where a great feast was waiting for them. There they were to live happily ever after.

The dream weaver vanished as mysteriously as he had appeared, but because of her penny thread, Selena was never cold or hungry ever again.

SANTA'S BEST COAT

It was Christmas Eve and the Head Gnome at the Gnometown Cleaners had just finished pressing Santa Claus's best red coat. "All those soot marks have come off," he said to the Smallest Gnome, as he brushed the white fur round the collar. "Now it looks as good as new."

The Head Gnome folded the coat carefully and put it in a large cardboard box. "Now take this along to Santa Claus right away," he told the Smallest Gnome.

So the Smallest Gnome set off, carrying the box carefully. He had quite a long way to go and the box seemed to get heavier and heavier and heavier. "Oh dear," sighed the Smallest Gnome, as he walked through Winter Wood. "I do wish I could have a rest for a few minutes."

Then he saw a large, hollow tree. "Just the place," he said to himself. "It will be sheltered from the wind in there." So he squeezed

GNOMETOWN CLEANERS

through the hole into the tree. Then he put down the box and sat on a pile of dry leaves.

The Smallest Gnome only meant to rest for a little while, but soon he felt very drowsy and fell asleep.

Much higher in the tree lived Sammy Squirrel and he was curled up on his bed of dry leaves. Suddenly he began to shiver. "It's getting much colder," said Sammy. "I really need some more

bedclothes."

So he jumped out of bed and looked out of his front door. "Goodness, it's beginning to snow," he cried. "I had better go and get some more dry leaves."

Sammy scurried down the tree trunk and hopped through the hole at the bottom. There he saw the Smallest Gnome, fast asleep. "Someone else is using my bedclothes," sighed Sammy. "What shall I do?"

Then he saw the box which the Smallest Gnome had put on the ground. He lifted the lid and saw Santa's best red coat. "This will be much warmer than leaves," chuckled Sammy, and he slipped in between the folds of the coat and pulled the lid back over him.

After a while the Smallest Gnome woke up. "Oh dear, it's getting dark," he gasped. "I shall have to hurry or Santa won't have his best red coat back in time to

wear it tonight.

He looked out of the hollow tree and saw the snow, which was getting really deep. Then he saw something moving through the wood towards him.

It was Rudolph, Santa's reindeer. "Santa sent me to fetch his best red coat," called Rudolph. "He's been waiting for it all afternoon. Where have you been?"

"I fell asleep," confessed the Smallest Gnome."

"Dear me," said Rudolph, shaking his head. "You'd better ride on my back or Santa will be late starting tonight."

So the Smallest Gnome lifted the box onto Rudolph's back. "It's heavier than ever," he puffed, not knowing that Sammy Squirrel was curled up inside.

Off they trotted, through the wood, until at last they saw the lights shining through the windows of Santa's house. Santa himself was waiting by the open door, in his

waiting by the open door, in his shirtsleeves. "Have you cleaned my coat well?" he asked.

"Oh, yes," replied the Smallest Gnome, putting the box on the table and opening the lid.

"Goodness me, whoever is this?" cried Santa. Sammy Squirrel lay curled up on the coat, still fast asleep.

"Wake up!" called Santa. "We'll have to take you back to the wood."

So Santa put on his best red coat, and Sammy and the Smallest Gnome climbed on the sledge with him. First, Santa took Sammy Squirrel back to his tree house in Winter Wood and gave him a cosy quilt from a doll's bed to keep him warm.

"Oh, thank you," murmured

Sammy, sleepily. "This will keep me warm for the rest of the winter."

Then Santa took the Smallest Gnome back to Gnometown and pulled a big parcel from the back of the sledge. "Perhaps this will help you to make your deliveries on time," he chuckled, as he drove away with Rudolph pulling his sledge over the snow.

"Thank you," called the
Smallest Gnome, waving until they
were out of sight. Then he quickly
pulled all the wrappings off the big
parcel.

Inside was a shiny new bicycle
with a big carrier basket on the
front. "It's just what I wanted!" cried

the Smallest Gnome, jumping on
and pedalling round and round with
excitement. "This will make my
work much easier."

So now the Smallest Gnome
can make his deliveries at top
speed, and Santa never has any
trouble getting his best red coat
back from the cleaners.

Gina The Giddy Giraffe

GO TO AFRICA

Gina the Giraffe had a long neck and long legs like all the other giraffes that lived in the zoo. She could reach up and nibble the food that the Giraffe Keeper put in a big rack above he head, just like all the other giraffes.

What Gina could not do was bend her head and drink from the pool like all the other giraffes. Every time Gina put her head down, she felt giddy.

So Gina had to drink water through a long straw. The straws had to be specially made and the Giraffe Keeper made an awful fuss about it. "Buying these special straws takes all my pocket money," he grumbled. "I don't know why you have to be different to all the other giraffes."

Lots of people came to the zoo to see all the animals and one day a visitor dropped a book near the Giraffe House. By stretching out her long neck, Gina could just see the picture on the cover. It showed a lovely, sunny place and underneath were the words: "Go to Africa for your holidays".

"I'd like to go to Africa for *my* holidays," said Gina.

"Don't be silly," said the other giraffes. "How ever would you get there?"

That very day the Zoo Manager came round and started counting all the giraffes. "The people who live near here are complaining about the noise the animals make," he told the Giraffe Keeper. "So we are going to move the zoo to another place. We shall have to take all the animals in special trucks."

"How exciting," said Gina. "Perhaps not as exciting as going to Africa, but at least I shall see a bit of the world."

All the other giraffes grumbled at having to move and only Gina really looked forward to it.

At last the day came when all the special trucks drove into the zoo and the keepers began loading the animals into them. Some animals made an awful fuss about getting inside and Gina began to feel very annoyed. "We shall never get away at this rate," she sighed.

At last some special trucks drew up outside the Giraffe House. They had open tops because the giraffes had such long necks. Gina went into the very last truck. "Hooray," she cried, "now we're off!"

Crowds of people gathered along the road because it was a very strange sight to see. The animals went right through the town and out into the country. At last they stopped at a place where there was a very low bridge. "The giraffes will have to put their heads down while we drive through," said one truck driver.

So the giraffes lowered their heads. All except Gina. She could not put her head down because she was afraid of feeling giddy. "What shall we do about Gina?" asked the Giraffe Keeper. "She always has to be different."

He was getting really cross about it and Gina was almost in tears, when along came a big lorry. It couldn't get by because Gina was blocking the way.

"What's the trouble?" asked the driver, climbing out of his cab.

"We can't move because of our giddy giraffe," said the Giraffe Keeper. "Gina can't go under the bridge because she won't put her head down."

"Perhaps we could could get her over the bridge," suggested the lorry driver.

There was a big machine on the back of the lorry and Gina couldn't guess what it was. But the lorry driver started an engine, pressed a button and part of the machine began to rise up into the air. It was a huge crane.

Gina's keeper tied some ropes around her and then hooked the ropes to the crane. Gina rose slowly into the air. "This is exciting," she said, "only I do hope they don't drop me."

The crane lifted Gina right over the bridge and lowered her gently down on the other side. As soon as her feet touched the ground, the Giraffe Keeper untied the ropes. Then he stopped to chat to the lorry driver.

He was gone so long that Gina started to wander along by the side of a river, nibbling at the trees as she felt rather hungry. Then she saw a big barge tied by the riverside. She decided to take a closer look.

As Gina stepped off the river bank and onto the barge, one foot got caught in the mooring line. She gave a kick to free her leg and the line broke. Before she could turn round, Gina was sailing down the river.

"This makes a nice change from that bumpy truck," she said, not feeling at all worried. But after a while the barge began to rock from side to side and looking down at the water, Gina saw big waves all around her. She was floating out to sea.

A seagull swooped down and settled on the barge. "You'd better watch out," he warned. "There's bad weather ahead."

He poked around the wrecked barge and found a red spotted hanky, and tied it round Gina's neck like a flag.

"Wave your neck if you see a boat," he told Gina.

"Oh, dear," cried Gina, feeling very scared. "I can't stop the barge. What shall I do?"

"I'll keep a look-out for you," said the seagull. So he flew onto Gina's head and they sailed on through the stormy seas. The sky grew darker and the waves grew bigger, and Gina closed her eyes tightly.

"Land ahoy!" squawked the seagull. "Look out, or we'll run right into it."

The next minute there was a big crash, Gina opened her eyes and found they had been shipwrecked on a small island. "What shall I do now?" she asked the seagull.

"You'd better show a distress signal," said the seagull.

Soon they heard the sound of an engine. "Is it a boat?" asked Gina.
"No, it's a helicopter," said the seagull, looking up at the sky.

The helicopter pilot could hardly believe his eyes when he saw Gina's
distress signal. He flew down and went round and round the island. "That
helicopter is making me feel dizzy," complained Gina.

The helicopter flew off and after a while she saw a lifeboat coming
towards the island. "Hooray, I'm going to be rescued," she cried excitedly.

But when the lifeboat arrived, Gina found she was much too big to go
on it. "We'll have to make a raft," decided the lifeboatmen.

So they took some planks from the wrecked barge and tied them
together. Then Gina stepped onto it and they towed her across the water

until she could see land again, though it was different from any land she had seen before.

"It's just like the picture I saw in that book at the zoo," she cried. "I do believe this is Africa!"

As soon as she was safely ashore, Gina thanked the lifeboatmen and said goodbye to the seagull. Then she ran into the jungle.

As she was nibbling a tasty leaf from one of the trees, she saw a monkey sitting on a branch. "I'm very thirsty after my adventures," Gina told him. "But I don't suppose you've any special straws here in the jungle. How can I drink without getting giddy?"

"I'll show you," replied the monkey, and he led Gina through the jungle to a big waterfall.

Gina found she could drink as much as she liked without bending her head and feeling giddy. "This is lovely," she said. "I do like Africa, so I am going to stay here for a very long holiday!"

The Dog Who Fetched Father Christmas

Mr. and Mrs Banks, their son, Matthew, and his little dog, Teddy, were on their way to spend Christmas on the farm with Matt's grandparents.

Teddy loved riding in the car. He would pad up and down on the back seat, first looking out of one side of the car and then the other. Mr. and Mrs Banks sat in the front singing 'The Twelve Days of Christmas'. Everyone was in a jolly mood, except Matt.

"Come on, Matt, why don't you join in?" said his mother. But Matt stayed silent.

Teddy stopped padding up and down and looked at his master. Something was wrong. He had never seen him look so glum.

"Cheer up," said his father. "After all it is Christmas."

"Then why can't we have it at home?"

Mr. and Mrs Banks were astonished to hear what their son had said. "I don't understand," said his mother, "when we told you we were spending Christmas at the farm you were thrilled and couldn't wait for the holiday to come."

Matt mumbled something about Father Christmas.

"What about Father Christmas?" asked his mother.

"How will he know where I am?"

His parents looked puzzled. Matt went on.

"How will he know where to leave my presents if I'm at the farm? When we wrote my letter telling him what I wanted for Christmas we put our address on it. He'll go to the house and if I'm not there he'll take my presents away again."

His parents smiled at each other. "Father Christmas will know where to find you, you can be sure of that," they told him.

But Matt wasn't convinced, and neither was Teddy.

When they arrived at the farm Matt cheered up a little. There were hugs and kisses from his grandparents then everyone tucked into a delicious farmhouse supper. Afterwards they played card games in front of a roaring fire until it was time for Matt to go to bed. He kissed everyone goodnight then headed for the door.

"Haven't you forgotten something?" said Granny. Matt stopped and frowned.

"Aren't you going to hang up your stocking ready for Father Christmas?" Matt shook his head.

His mother sighed. "He thinks that because he's not at home, Father Christmas won't know where to leave his presents."

"What nonsense," laughed Granny. "Of course Father Christmas will know where you are."

"That's what we told him," said Mr. Banks.

Half-heartedly, Matt helped Granny hang up his stocking - a large woolly sock with darns in the toe and heel - and then went to bed. Teddy went with him and settled down by Matt's feet. He listened to Matt sniffing back his

tears before dropping off to sleep. Teddy stayed wide awake, thinking.

He thought how miserable Matt would be if he woke up in the morning with no presents to unwrap and play with and he decided to do something about it. He would go back to the house,

wait for the sleigh to come, and then fetch Father Christmas to the farm.

He slipped off the bed and went downstairs. The grown-ups were looking through an old photograph album and didn't notice the little dog make his way to the door. It was shut tight. He hid behind a curtain deciding what to do.

Just then Grandpa got up to go out and check all the animals. He put on his big coat and boots, said, "Shan't be long", and opened the door. Teddy scooted out between Grandpa's legs leaving him wondering whether he'd seen something or not.

Over the fields he went in what he hoped was the direction of the motorway, but in the dark it all seemed different and strange. It was also starting to snow.

On and on he ran until his paws were sore. He was beginning to think he had chosen the wrong direction when, on reaching the top of a hill, he found himself gazing at the bright lights and the wide lanes of the motorway. He gave a bark of

He had a couple of goes, but each time he slithered back to the ground. Then he heard the engine start up. Teddy hurled himself into the air, cleared the tailboard and fell into the lorry just as it was moving off. Bruised but pleased with himself, Teddy settled down for the ride.

When the lorry slowed down, Teddy guessed that they had left the motorway and poked out his nose for a look around. The streets looked familiar so he decided to get off. He scrambled to the top of the tailboard, balanced there for a moment then leaped into the air, landing flat in the road. In the distance he heard the faint sound of jingling bells. He picked himself up and hurried on.

Turning a corner he could see Santa's sleigh hovering over his house. When he got there he could hear moving about inside so he scratched at the front door. There was no answer, so he scratched again. When that was ignored he barked, very loudly. The door was opened in a trice by a red-coated, white-bearded gentleman who seemed to be rather cross.

"What do you think you're doing?" he hissed. "I'll never deliver all these presents by morning if you wake everyone up."

Teddy took hold of his red coat and tried to pull him out the door.

"Wouldn't it be easier if you told me what you want. I can understand you, you know."

Teddy stopped tugging and started talking.

"I see," said Father Christmas, when Teddy had finished. "So, if your master's not here, where is he?"

"Wuff," wuffed Teddy. "Wuff, wuff, wuff. Wuff, wuff."

joy and slid down the snowy bank to the lay-by below.

A lorry was parked there and Teddy decided to get a lift. The back of the lorry was open but high up. He would have to jump.

"Then I'd better be off. By the way, would you like a lift?"

Teddy wagged his tail. He'd been wondering how he would get
back to the farm. Tucked up under a warm rug on the seat of
Santa's sleigh, he went fast asleep.

When he woke up he was surprised to find himself back at the
bottom of Matt's bed. It was morning and Matt was still asleep.

"Wuff," barked Teddy. "Wuff, wuff." 'Time to get up, lazybones,'
he was saying. 'Don't you know it's Christmas Day?'

"All right," said Matt, drowsily, "I'll get up. But I don't know why
you're so excited. Father Christmas won't have been. I know it."

"I wouldn't be so sure of that." Matt's mother was standing in

the doorway, a big smile on her face.

Matt leaped out of bed and tore downstairs, Teddy at his heels. They nearly fell over each other getting into the sitting room.

Matt's stocking was bulging with toys, sweets, fruit and nuts and on the floor were several brightly wrapped parcels. Hanging next to Matt's stocking was another smaller one. Inside it was a rubber bone, a new collar and some doggy treats. How it had got there puzzled everyone except Matt and Teddy.

"Thank you, Father Christmas," yelled Matt.

"Wuff, wuff, wuff, wuff," went Teddy, which meant exactly the same thing.

Olly Octopus and the Sea King's Treasure

King Neptune, who rules all the seas, sent for the Captain of his Fish Guard. "I have a special chest of treasure to be guarded and I want you to put your best soldier on the job," he commanded.

"I'll put Olly Octopus on guard duty," decided the Captain. "With his eight arms he can easily capture any thief who tries to steal the King's treasure.

So Olly had to keep watch on the cave where the treasure chest was kept. Inside the chest was the King's best crown. There were also lots of pearl necklaces that the Mermaid Princesses wore when visitors came to the palace.

At first all was quiet, but then some oysters popped into the cave. "Can we see the Princesses' pearls?" they asked.

"Certainly not," said Olly, who was afraid the oysters might trick him and make off with the pearls. So he glared at them and the oysters hurried away.

Then a lobster came along. "Let me try on the King's crown, Olly," he begged.

"Certainly not," replied Olly. He was afraid the lobster would hold on to the crown, once he got it in his claws. "Go away," said Olly, sternly.

Then Olly saw two very strange-looking fish swimming towards the cave. They were divers, wearing underwater masks and carrying sharp looking harpoons. "I'll hide until they've gone," Olly decided.

The divers saw the treasure chest and tried to lift it, but it was too heavy. So they swam away and Olly followed them up and up through the water, until he could see the bottom of the boat.

"We've found a treasure chest," he heard the divers say, as they scrambled on board. "It's very heavy, so it must be full of gold. We need a long cable to haul it up."

Olly swam back to the cave as fast as he could. "I've got to do something quickly," he gasped, scratching his head with one of his eight arms.

Then he had an idea. He turned the key of the chest and, lifting the lid, quickly put the crown and all the necklaces over his arms. Then he filled the chest with stones, locked it, took the key and hid behind a rock.

He was just in time, because a moment later the divers came back with a long cable. They hooked it onto the chest and the sailors on the boat began to pull it. "Now we shall all be rich!" they cried as they pulled the chest on board.

They broke open the lock and lifted the lid. What a shock they had when they saw the chest held nothing but stones. They got very angry with the divers and began throwing all the stones overboard.

Olly heard the stones thumping down on the sand outside the cave. Then there was an extra big THUMP! and the empty chest came down, too.

Olly put the crown and all the necklaces back in the chest, because his arms were aching with all that weight. "The lock will have to be mended," he chuckled, "but the treasure is safe."

The Captain of the Fish Guard was so pleased about the way Olly's quick thinking had saved the treasure that he promoted him to sergeant. Then all the Mermaid Princesses sewed stripes on eight special armbands for Sergeant Olly Octopus.

Santa's Ride

"Christmas is coming!"
    A whisper had stirred
Mice in the meadow.
    A half-awake bird
Peeped from its shelter
    where berries hung bright,
Saw the moon rising
    to shed her pale light
Over the country
    and over the town
Where, through the day,
    the soft snow drifting down
Covered the land;
    now a mantle of white
Sparkled with frost
    in the hush of the night.

Stockings were hung
    at the foot of each bed,
Waiting for Santa
    to come with his sled;
Each sleepy head
    to its pillow had flown:
"Christmas is coming!"
    the whisper had grown.
Louder it blew
    over sea, over shore,
Santa could hear it
    and lingered no more:
"Away now, my beauties,"
    he called to his deer,
Climbing his sledge
    with its load of good cheer.

"Christmas is coming!"
    the waves of the sea
Echoed the bells
    as they rang merrily;
Mice in the meadow
    saw Santa pass by,
Birds sang their greetings
    that reached to the sky.
Santa heard all
    as he made his long ride,
Stars for his lanterns,
    the moon for his guide
Lighting his way
    to each cottage and house,
Silent as snowfall,
    as soft as a mouse.

Letters to Santa
    had asked him to bring
Cycles and spaceships,
    a doll that can sing;
Here a small cradle
    and there a big train,
Toy bears and tea sets,
    a car or a plane.
Nothing, it seemed,
    was too large or too small;
Santa, at last,
    had delivered them all.
Nobody spied him,
    so fast had he sped,
Leaving his toys
    at the foot of each bed.

Only the mice
      in the meadow had seen,
Only the birds
      in the holly bush green;
When the young dreamers
      with morning awoke,
Giving their stockings
      a prod or a poke.

Quickly they tumbled
      from bed to the floor
Wide-eyed with wonder
      at toys in galore.
Then they all shouted
      and gave a big cheer:
"Hooray for Santa,
      now Christmas is here!"

A Picture To Paint

The Little Rabbit and The Forgetful Elf

Little Rabbit put her nose out of the burrow and looked round. The sky was blue and the sun was shining.

"So what if it is winter," she thought. "It's too nice to stay inside." And without a word to anyone she slipped out and ran around chasing shadows until she saw some other small animals enjoying the winter sun and joined them.

Not far away, someone else was giving thought to the winter weather - the Chief Weather Elf, who had called together his elves for a meeting.

"It is winter," he began, "but some of the younger animals are still out playing whereas, by now, they should be sleeping until the Spring. A chilly wind and some snow are what are needed. So off you go," he said, clapping his hands and making the elves jump to their feet. "And don't forget what you are supposed to be doing," he added, looking at one elf in particular.

Elvin knew why the Chief was staring at him. He happened to be rather forgetful and often got into trouble because of it.

He once forgot to make it rain on Bluebell Wood and the flowers nearly died of thirst. Then in the Autumn he left the leaves on the trees. When he remembered that they weren't supposed to be there he made them fall all at once and buried some animals who were passing at the time. They were very cross - and so was the Chief.

Elvin knew he'd better not make any mistakes this time and flew off, determined to do the job properly. But he hadn't flown far when he spotted a pixie he hadn't seen for a long time and flew down for a chat.

The other weather elves were already doing their job; a chilly wind was blowing and flakes of snow were floating to earth. One landed on Little Rabbit's nose and melted. She had never seen snow before and kept trying to catch it. Her friends, though, were starting to feel cold and were scampering to their homes.

Little Rabbit shivered. "Perhaps I'd better go home too. But which way is home?" The wind was blowing the snow about and she could hardly see. She set off, not knowing whether it was the right or wrong direction.

The forgetful elf was saying goodbye to his friend and thinking how much he'd enjoyed his chat when a funny feeling came over him. It was the feeling he got when he knew he'd forgotten something.

"Now what was it I was supposed to do?" He scratched his ear and thought hard. "A shower of rain? No, that was yesterday. A strong wind to blow away the leaves? No, that was weeks ago." Then he remembered. "Snow! I have to make it snow!" And off he flew.

Little Rabbit had made her way into the wood. By now the ground was thickly covered and she was feeling so cold that she could hardly put one paw in front of another. She sank deeper into the snow and icy tears trickled down her nose.

Then she noticed something rather odd a little way ahead of her. It was a patch of green in the middle of all the snow.

"If I can get to it," she thought, "I'll be safe until someone finds me." And she crawled through the snow to the little clearing where she lay down, exhausted.

Elvin was flying overhead. He was about to throw down a handful of snow from the big sack he was carrying when he spotted Little Rabbit. He could see that she was wet and shivering and he knew that if he made it snow no one would ever find her.

He didn't know what to do. The Chief would be making his rounds soon, checking that all the elves had done their work. If he came to the wood and found a big, snowless patch, Elvin knew he'd be in terrible trouble. He might be taken off weather duty and put onto ground work; looking after plants and flowers. Elvin shuddered at the thought. He hated gardening.

He let a few flakes fall from his hand, but that was all. He sighed, put the rest back in his bag and sat in a tree hoping that someone would come and rescue Little Rabbit before the Chief found him.

He didn't have to wait long.

"What do you think you are doing?" said a stern voice. "I knew you were forgetful, but this is sheer disobedience and must be punished. You will have your flying powers taken away and be put onto ground work."

Elvin groaned.

Just as the Chief was flying off, he noticed a large rabbit making its way across the snow. When it caught sight of Little Rabbit in the clearing it moved as quickly as it could to get to her.

The elves watched anxiously as the rabbit shook and prodded the lifeless bundle and tried to warm her. It seemed as if he had got there too late.

Then there was a tiny movement and Little Rabbit opened her eyes and smiled at her father who picked her up in his mouth and carried her back across the snow to their warm burrow.

The Chief cleared his throat. "It seems that your forgetfulness has saved that little rabbit's life so I will not punish you this time. But in future you must remember things. Try tying a piece of twine around your finger to remind you," he suggested.

Elvin took the Chief's advice and went about with little bits of twine tied around every finger. The trouble was, he couldn't remember why he'd put them there!

The No Snowman

"Roses still blooming in December, whoever heard of such a thing?"
exclaimed Granny Bates, looking out into the garden. "When I was a girl
I'd have been out there building a snowman by now."

"I can remember it snowing once," said her grandson, Joe, "but it all
melted before I could go out and play in it," he added, sadly.

His younger sister, Polly, climbed onto her grandma's lap. "Tell me
about the snowman, Granny," she begged.

"Oh, there were lots of them," she explained. "Me and my brother would
make one each winter it snowed. But there was one in particular that I
remember. It stayed in the garden for days and days and then, when it
began to thaw, it melted ever so slowly until it was a tiny snowball in the
middle of the grass."

"I want to make a snowman like that," said Polly. "I want to make it now."

"Well you can't," her brother told her, "there's no snow." Being a few years older than his sister he was much more practical.

Mr. Bates walked in and Polly jumped off her grandma's lap and rushed up to him. "I want to make a snowman, Daddy. Please can I? Oh, please, please!"

"That might be rather difficult, seeing as how there's no snow about," he laughed.

"That's what I said," chipped in Joe.

Mr. Bates scratched his head and thought for a moment. "Tell you what, why don't you make a No-Snowman instead?"

Polly thought it was a wonderful idea, but Joe was more cautious.

"How do we make a No-Snowman?" he asked.

"Wait until tomorrow and you'll see," was all their father would say.

The next day, wearing their warmest clothes, for it had turned quite cold, Polly and Joe joined their father in the garden. He had been rummaging in his tool shed and had brought out a couple of old sacks, one big, one small. He proceeded to fill them up with all sorts of garden rubbish until they were two fat shapes. Then Mr. Bates stuck the small one on top of the big one so that it vaguely looked like a head on a body.

"There, that's my work done. It's up to you to finish him off," he told them and went indoors.

Polly and Joe looked first at the oddly shaped sacks and then at each other.

"What shall we do now?" said Polly.

"I don't know," answered Joe, grumpily. "Whoever heard of a No-Snowman any way? I'm going in."

"No!" cried Polly, grabbing at his coat. "You're to stay and help me, Daddy said."

"No he didn't. Now let me go."

"No!" screamed his sister, holding on tight.

Joe yanked his coat out of Polly's hands and she sat down on the ground with a bump. "I'm going to tell Mummy you pushed me," she said, scrambling up.

"Hello, you two," said a neighbour, popping her head over the fence. "What's that you've got there?"

"It's a No-Snowman," mumbled Joe, rather embarrassed.

"A No-Snowman? That's a clever idea. Hang on, I think I've got something he can wear." She disappeared and returned carrying an old overcoat which she passed over the fence.

"Thanks," said Polly and Joe, as they draped the coat around the sack and did up the buttons. It was a perfect fit.

Their grandma suddenly appeared with a pair of woollen gloves which they tucked up into the sleeves. The No-Snowman now had hands. Polly and Joe stood back to look at him. From behind they heard a giggle. They were being watched by some children from down the road.

"What's that?" they called.

"It's a funny kind of scarecrow," joked one.

"Bit late for Guy Fawkes night," jeered another.

Joe didn't know what to say. These were the people he went to school with and he knew they'd make fun of him if he told them what it really was.

Then Polly spoke. "Actually, it's a No-Snowman," she said in a rather

grand voice.

There was a silence, then a boy shouted, "A No-Snowman, what a great idea. Can we help?" And without waiting for a reply they rushed off, shortly to return with scarves, hats, an umbrella and even a pair of boots for the funny sack man.

They were a noisy crowd and soon the garden was filled with shouting and laughing as they argued about which scarf looked best and how he should wear his hat.

"I like making a No-Snowman," yelled Polly.

A cheer went up as Mrs Bates arrived with a tray of hot chocolate and biscuits, but it was quickly followed with a groan when she pointed out that the No-Snowman hadn't got a face. No-one could think of how to make him one.

"Buttons!" cried Polly and Joe's mother, as she dashed into the house and came out with her sewing box and some strong glue. She stuck on two blue buttons for the eyes, a pink button for the nose and four red ones for the mouth. She made him look as though he was smiling.

"Now he's finished what are you going to call him?"

The children got into a huge argument over his name and Polly's voice could be heard above the rest, crying, "But he's my No-Snowman, so I should choose the name."

Then everyone went quiet when something most unexpected happened. It started to snow, slowly at first and then thick and fast until it covered the ground.

The children from down the road stamped and yelled. "We're off to make a proper snowman. We don't want your silly No-Snowman anymore." And away they went, taking their scraves and hats and all the other things

they'd brought.

Polly and Joe suddenly felt cold and went inside.

That afternoon the children from down the road built their snowman. Polly and Joe could see it from the upstairs window.

"We could go out and make one too, if you like," offered Joe.

Polly shook her head. "No thanks. I think I like our No-Snowman best."

"So do I," agreed Joe. "And at least he'll still be there when it's thawed. He'll last for even longer than the one Granny made."

The words had barely left Joe's lips than the sun came out and shone warmly. In no time at all the thick blanket had become a few snowy patches and the 'proper' snowman was just a little white pile.

The No-Snowman still stood proud and smiling in the corner of the garden and while other winters and other snowmen came and went, he stayed there for a long, long time.